Mr. Little's NOISY TRAIN

Richard Fowler

Grosset & Dunlap

ISBN 0-448-19212-8   B C D E F G H I

A Ventura book, designed and produced by Ventura Publishing Ltd.,
11-13 Young Street, London W8 5EH, England.
Color origination, printing, and binding by Tien Wah Press (Pte) Ltd., Singapore.

Mr. Little was about
to take his freight train
out of the railroad yard.
Suddenly he heard scraping
and fluttering noises
coming from the front
of the engine.
He opened the smokebox
door and found . . .

Tieplate

Tie

Coal tender

Cab roof

Cab lookouts

Safety valves

Whistle

Steam dome

Smokestack

Handrail

Boiler

Side water tank

Smokebox

flutter

scrape

flutter

Smokebox door

Cab door

Nameboard

BILLY

Cab deck

Sand box

Lamp hanger

Main brake pipe

Bumper

Drive axle

Pilot coupler

Driving wheel

Brake shoe

Pilot beam

Wheel guard

Rail

TR 153
1007651

"Who's there?" called
Mr. Little when he heard a
huffing and puffing sound
coming from inside the cab.
He climbed up the steps
and carefully opened
the firebox door.
Inside he found . . .

Brake control

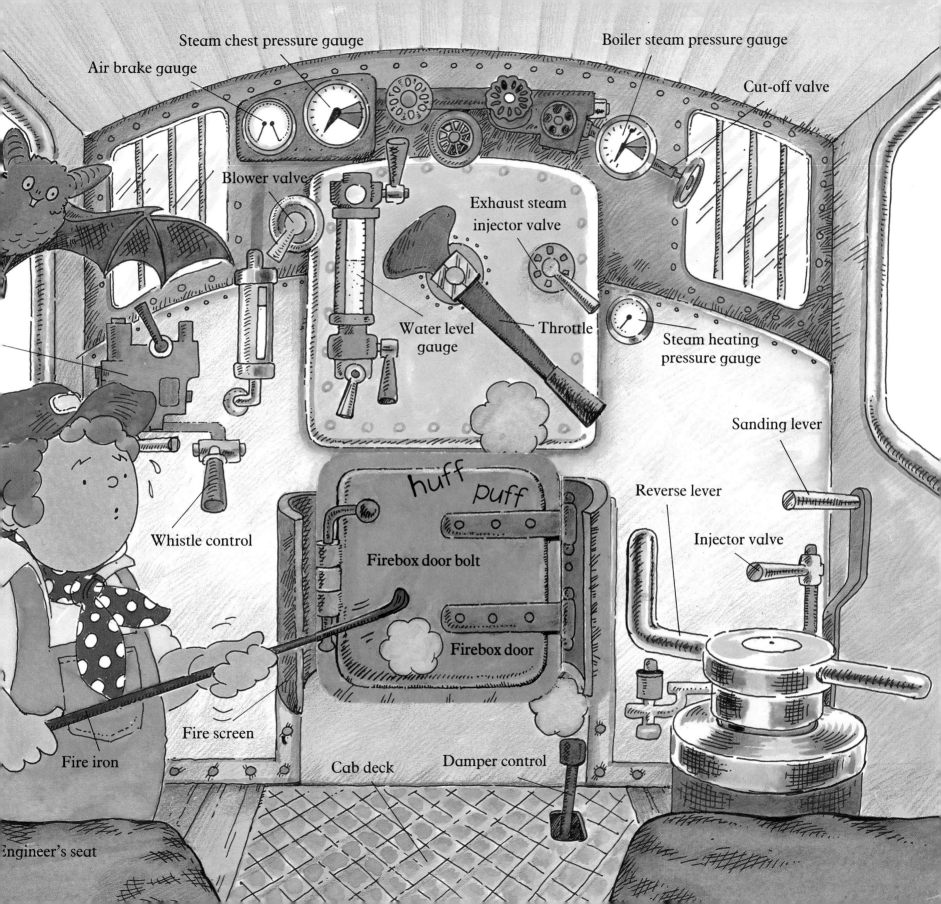

Air brake gauge

Steam chest pressure gauge

Boiler steam pressure gauge

Cut-off valve

Blower valve

Exhaust steam injector valve

Water level gauge

Throttle

Steam heating pressure gauge

Sanding lever

Reverse lever

Injector valve

Whistle control

huff puff

Firebox door bolt

Firebox door

Fire screen

Fire iron

Cab deck

Damper control

Engineer's seat

From the refrigerator car
behind the engine
came slithering and
clonking noises.
"What's going on?"
exclaimed Mr. Little.
He quickly opened
the door and found . . .

Electric fans

Gutter

Grille

slither

clonk

slither

clonk

ICE

Refrigeration unit

Ice cube

Brake shoe

Flange

Wheel

Axle

"We'll never leave on time!" moaned Mr. Little as he heard strange humming and grating sounds coming from the hopper car. Mr. Little opened the door and found . . .

Melted ice

Sand and ballast

Hopper

SAND

Hopper
door control

hum
grate

Hand brake

Hopper door

Leaf spring

Chute

Splashing and gurgling sounds
came from inside the
tank car. "Now what?"
asked Mr. Little
as he climbed up
the ladder.
He opened the hatch
and to his surprise
found . . .

From the caboose at the rear
of the train came muffled
whistling and flapping sounds.
"I don't believe this!"
cried Mr. Little.
He opened the door . . .

Air vents

Conductor's lookout

Gutter

whistle

flap

flap

flap

whistle

Handrail

Tail
lamp

Wheel

Flange

With a clink-clank-clunk the train started to move. *So did Mr. Little!* He ran past the owl,

the alligator, the desert rat,
the polar bear, the penguin, the dragon,
and the bat . . .

and jumped onto the engine
just in time!
Then with a scrape, a flutter,
a huff and a puff,
a slither, a clonk,
a splash and a gurgle,
a whistle, a clink-clank-clunk,
and a very loud . . .

Switch

Switch point

Tracks